This book belongs to:

....

Thomas and Bertie

The Rev. W. Awdry

One day, Thomas was at a
junction, when Bertie the Bus
came into view.
"I can go faster than you," boasted
Thomas, letting off steam.

"OK, I'll race you," said Bertie.
The Drivers agreed and in a flash they were off.
Thomas puffed loudly as he pulled away from the
station.

Thomas hurried along as quickly as he could.
But Bertie was too fast!
"He's a long way ahead! A long way ahead!"
called Annie and Clarabel.

Then Bertie had to stop at a level crossing and Thomas sailed by!
"Goodbye, Bertie!" he shouted as he whooshed past.

"Hurry! Hurry! Hurry!" panted Thomas as he headed towards the bridge.
Then he whistled in surprise as Bertie crossed in front of him!

At the next station, the signal was up and Thomas
had to stop.
"Oh dear, oh dear," he gasped.

The signal soon changed and Thomas rumbled
over the bridge.
There was Bertie stuck at a red light!
"We'll beat Bertie yet!" Thomas puffed.

Suddenly, the lights changed and Bertie shot
ahead, tooting loudly.
"Quick! Quick! Quick!" urged Annie and Clarabel,
and soon Thomas and Bertie were racing alongside
each other.

But when Thomas reached his full speed,
Bertie just wasn't fast enough.
Thomas raced ahead into a tunnel, leaving
Bertie behind.

Thomas raced through the last tunnel,
as Bertie struggled up the steep hill.
Thomas whooshed into the station, whistling
proudly, "I've done it, hurrah!"

The passengers shouted,
"Three cheers for Thomas!"
and when Bertie came in
they cheered him too.
"Well done, Thomas," said
Bertie. "You are a Really
Useful Engine!"

Thomas' Birthday

Today it is Thomas' birthday! Henry is rushing to
Thomas' party, when he has to stop by the circus.
Hooosh! Henry let's off steam and frightens one of
the elephants.
Whoosh! The elephant squirts water all over
Henry in return. Poor Henry will have to get dry
again for the party!

Percy is going to Thomas' party, too. But as he is passing the harbour, he decides to have a look at the sea. His trucks bump him forward so that he is closer to the water.

SMASH! Oh, dear. The trucks have bumped him too hard and he falls into the water.
The Fat Controller is not pleased with Percy.
"You are a very silly engine," he says. "Now you might be late for Thomas' party."

James is in a fix. On the way to the party, the naughty trucks push him much too fast and his brakes don't work. He can't stop!
CRASH! The workmen find him stuck in a field of cows.
"Help!" he whistles. "I hope I get to Thomas' party on time."

Thomas is so excited about his birthday party
that he can't stop rushing. By the time he arrives
at the viaduct, he is very hot and thirsty.
"We'll have to stop and get some water, Thomas,"
says his Driver. "Let's hope it doesn't make you
late for your own birthday party!"

Luckily, Percy, Henry and James have all arrived at Thomas' party safe and sound. When Thomas puffs into the station, everyone cheers.

"I didn't think you would get here on time," says The Fat Controller. "But you are a Really Useful Engine after all. Happy birthday, Thomas!"